FriesenPress

Suite 300 - 990 Fort St
Victoria, BC, V8V 3K2
Canada

www.friesenpress.com

ISBN
978-1-03-910604-8 (Hardcover)
978-1-03-910603-1 (Paperback)
978-1-03-910605-5 (eBook)

1. JUVENILE FICTION, ANIMALS, HORSES

Distributed to the trade by The Ingram Book Company

The LEGEND of STORM

ALICE RADOUX

This book is dedicated to the memory of
Maurice Radoux (1935-2005) "The Other Half"

Maurice on Old Smoke

CHAPTER I
The Birth of a Legend

The peons still talk about it today. It became a legend. The story of Storm and how he saved the valley and señor Miguel's ranchero.

Over a hundred years ago, in a secluded valley of the towering Sierra Madre mountains, the ranchero of señor Miguel Delgado was prospering. Clear running brooks, high timber, and rolling lower reaches of the mountains that were ideal for cattle surrounded his ranchero. The sheep grew fat and woolly on the high slopes. The gamma grass on the valley floor was lush with protein, providing the best feed for the señor's Arabians. His purebred horses were known extensively and his foals were in great demand, bringing large sums.

The peons and vaqueros working for señor Miguel were humble, pious folk. They did their work with pride and contentment. Their children romped in the sun—carefree and full of wonder as all was well with their world.

The hacienda was long and low with many windows and was filled with large airy rooms. The front veranda, which ran the full length of the house, was shaded by long, green vines. In the summer the birds nested there, all day their music could be heard throughout the home. The courtyard was enclosed by a low adobe wall, yet the grass grew thick from the constant spray of the fountains. The mountains and timber formed a backdrop for the hacienda, which overlooked the valley.

To the east one could see the stables of the señor's prized Arabians. Built of thick adobe with oversized windows, inside the stable was cool and peaceful. The box stalls that lined the alleyway were roomy, and the packed clay floors were thickly covered with fresh straw. Near the entrance was a room for stable equipment and riding gear; the clean, polished leather gleamed in the sunlight as it streamed through the windows.

In the largest stall was the majestic El Baroun, sire of all the foals on the señor's ranchero. He stood fifteen hands tall and was steel grey. His small ears, which were pricked until almost touching, mirrored his alertness. His deep brown eyes glowed with an inner fire and his dish-shaped face and flaring nostrils proclaimed that here was a horse indeed: a royal Arabian.

Further down the stable was a small, grey mare. This was the gentle Surur, señor Miguel's pride. Her head was low. She was restless as she was heavy with foal. Her time was near.

The señor's Arabians had an aristocratic pedigree. The lineage of El Baroun and Surur traced back for generations to the founding stock of the Arabian breed. Arabian pedigrees were recorded through the dams, and both led back to the family of Kehilan; the family to which the great Darley Arabian belonged.

The señor chose to raise and use Arabians because of their good disposition, intelligence, stamina, and speed; but most of all, for their willing and courageous hearts.

The lives of señor Miguel and his people were full. With the birth of Surur's foal (which the señor knew would be a colt) he already looked forward to winning the two-year-old race that was held each year in Chihuahua. The señor's nearest neighbour and greatest rival, Pedro Gomez, had won this race for the last four years. Señor Gomez could not offer comparable competition to a foal that would be born of Surur and El Baroun. Breeding would make this an exceptional colt. With the right training, he would be unbeatable; a champion worthy of his heritage.

One day in the spring of 1863, a great storm arose over the mountains and the valley. Thunder rolled, lightning flashed, darkness descended. The birds sought shelter in the orchards. The peons hurried from the fields. Stillness reigned. All was quiet in anticipation of the approaching storm. The wind howled, lightning reared its head and slashed at the sky like a furious stallion. Thunder reverberated through the mountains. A rumbling stampede grew louder and closer. The rain came down in torrents and tore at everything in its path, causing rivers to form that poured down the valley floor with an increasingly destructive force.

Within the stables, the fury of the storm passed in muted tones. Surur paced her stall, then turned, lowering herself to the straw with a deep groan. Time passed. Between the rolls of thunder, the little mare struggled to bring about the birth of her foal who she had carried for eleven months. The foal struggled, impatient, eager to be born. He was ready to leave this safe, warm place to move into the living world. Pain came and pressure. He was being pushed relentlessly forward. Then with a quick surge, he slid out into the darkness of the stall and was still. It was over. Surur scrambled to her feet, whirling to snap the cord that joined them. He would no longer be a part of her, but a separate individual. The mare began licking him, stripping him clean and dry.

The colt drew his first breath, loudly snorting his greeting to the world. The fires of his great ancestors burned in his heart. He was ready for this big, new world. He could feel his mother's rough tongue caressing him. He moved his head to nuzzle her. He tried to scramble up, and like all newborn foals, he was soon standing, his legs straddled out to brace himself.

Smelling his mother near, he nuzzled her again, instinct making him search until he found her teat. He began nursing greedily. Strength flowed into him from the life-giving energy of his mother's milk. Yet at the hacienda, all slept through the night, unaware of the drama of life enacted in the stables.

Close to dawn, the storm eased. As the sun crept over the Sierra Madres, everyone began to stir. The onslaught of the storm was over. The birds were out, chirping of the beautiful spring day. The señor stepped onto his veranda and drew a deep breath. He stood in silent thankfulness before the quiet peacefulness of his valley. He then went to the stables to check on Surur, murmuring to El Baroun as he passed his stall.

Immediately his horseman's eye noticed the flat flanks and the mussed condition of the mare's hair. Swinging his eyes, he was confronted by the sight of a long-legged foal. Going inside the stall, he talked steadily to the mare, reassuring her that he meant no harm to her baby. The foal showed no fear; his eyes flashed with the gleam of his sire.

His ears were pricked forward. Standing posed as though ready for action, his dish-shaped face and small muzzle added to the arrogant and aristocratic head of his proclaimed blood-lines for all to see. His body was fire red, his mane, tail, and legs coal black; the perfect blood bay. His body looked strong and well-formed. His legs long and clean-cut, showing signs of power and speed.

Señor Miguel paused, confused by this small colt. The first-born of Surur and the great El Baroun. Sire and dam were steel grey, yet this foal was a blood bay; a throwback to his ancestors of the Arabian deserts. Was this a sign of good luck or of bad? Only time would tell.

CHAPTER II
The Growth of the Legend

Surur and her colt were in the big pasture for mares with new foals. The grass grew thick to help the mares produce nourishing milk for their colts and fillies. The new foals learned to use their unwieldy legs to grow strong and healthy. The weeks passed slowly, but each day the son of Surur became steadier on his feet. The pasture echoed to the drumming of his small hooves as he raced up and down. It looked like he would explode from sheer high spirits in his curiosity of this new world. His red coat shone like living fire. His black fuzzy mane and tail flared with an ebony glow. The señor was proud of the colt's good looks and action, yet still unsure if his colour was a good or bad omen.

Everyone was thinking of a suitable name for this firstborn colt. Señor even offered a prize for the best name and many names were suggested. He decided on a name that was given to him by his foreman's son, Juan Hosiez. Juan said, "The colt should be called Storm for he was born to the sound of thunder and lightning." Storm grew strong and sleek. Storm, out of Surur by El Baroun.

The weeks blended together, and the fresh green days of spring faded into the lazy hotness of summer. From the beginning, Storm was ahead of his playfellows. He was bigger, always showing them a clean pair of heels when racing around the meadow. The señor watched, his doubts about the young colt lessening with each passing day.

The colt was handled daily by the señor and the señor's Arabian trainer. Storm was eased into training; he was petted gently and learned that there was nothing to fear from these strange two-legged animals. He was haltered. His feet were picked up one by one until he stood quietly for all of his handlings. Treated with gentleness, he trusted people. He grew and played, getting stronger and swifter as the months passed. At six-months-old, like all the foals, he was separated from his mother and put into a different pasture in the valley. For the first few days, he was lonesome and frightened, then he became accustomed to being without Surur. He began eating the new grass and drinking the cold, clear water in the spring. He was on his own now; he was growing up.

The colt grew and played in the pastures with his playmates while the señor went about his business on the ranchero. He was beginning to believe the colt would be good enough to run in the two-year-old race. Señor Miguel's neighbour, Pedro Gomez, came to see Storm. Señor Gomez had heard stories of the colt from the peons who worked for him. Having heard of the strength, swiftness, and beauty of this colt, he had come to see if the stories were true.

Señor Gomez arrived one day at noon, accompanied by some of his vaqueros. Señor Delgado greeted his friendly rival at the hacienda's gate and brought him to the house for a noonday meal.

"Well, Pedro, my friend," said the señor. "I know why you have come by at this busy time of year."

"Of course, I have come to see if all the stories about this miracle colt of yours are true!"

"Ahhh! They are not stories, I assure you," said the señor. "I will have my trainer bring the colt to the hacienda, you will see for yourself."

After dinner, the two gentlemen moved to the front veranda with tall, cool drinks as the señor sent for Storm.

"See for yourself. Is he not the finest colt in all the country? As he should be with El Baroun for a sire and Surur for a dam!"

Señor Gomez's eyes narrowed as he looked the young colt over from the tip of his ears to the end of his tail. He looked with the knowing eyes of a horseman. He saw the promise of speed and strength in the colt's deep chest, fine strong legs, short back, and powerful hindquarters.

"He is indeed a very fine colt, but where does he get his colour?" he asked.

The señor frowned, not answering this, as señor Gomez was quick to note.

"It does not matter what colour a colt is," said the señor, "this colt is going to win the race for me in Chihuahua, you wait and see."

"He looks like he should be able to run, I admit," said señor Gomez. "That colour could mean he is a throwback to his desert ancestors, who were noted for their wildness and unpredictable temperaments." He looked slyly at señor Delgado as he spoke.

The señor blanched, stubbornly not admitting such a possibility to his rival.

"He will run the race and he will win!" señor Delgado stated, almost too emphatically.

"I would not be too sure of that," señor Gomez said. "I have a black colt that will be running against him, and I believe my colt can beat yours."

"Ha, so you think," said the señor, "but with the breeding your colt has, compared to Storm's, it's very doubtful. I would bet all that I own that Storm will beat your colt in the race."

"I'll take that bet," said señor Gomez. "I'll bet my ranchero against yours; all of my stock and all of my horses against yours. Will you do the same? Is it a bet?"

Señor Delgado swallowed hard; he had not meant to be taken so literally when he had spoken. "Well, I don't…"

"It's your choice," said Pedro, but with a knowing look added, "but of course, if you are afraid to… "

The señor's pride flared at the word afraid. "I accept the bet!" he answered swiftly.

"That includes El Baroun and Surur, and all of your Arabians of course," said Gomez shrewdly.

The señor hesitated. El Baroun was his pride, but the gentle Surur was his love.

"You said you would bet all you own. Either back what you say or don't boast about a horse that you have no faith in," señor Gomez quickly replied when he saw señor Delgado hesitate.

"I will bet El Baroun, Surur, and all that I possess!" señor Delgado said evenly, knowing that Storm would not let him down.

So the fatal bet was made on that hot day of Storm's first year. It was a day that señor Delgado would live to bitterly regret. Yet, there was no going back as his word was given. Señor Gomez went home, highly amused at the way he had trapped his rival into wagering all that he owned in the heat of the moment. He was confident his colt could beat Storm when the time came. Then he would own this valley—the largest estate in all of Mexico. Best of all, he would own señor Delgado's Arabians, whose horses he had coveted for a long time.

Señor Delgado went into his house in a pensive frame of mind. Not for the world did he want to admit that the colour of Storm gave him doubt as to the nature of his heart. Storm's colouring was a true throwback to those desert Arabians, but only time would tell about his heart. The first stallions had been fierce horses indeed, with all the cunning wiles needed in their native desert home. Such ancestors Storm could revert to; their prepotency was so strong that it could outweigh the potency of El Baroun and Surur.

All unknowing, the young Storm grew and played. Summer passed and winter settled on the valley. It was a mild winter that went quickly, and soon the green grass of spring was growing again.

Now Storm began training intensely. As he approached the spring of his first year, he was started on the long-line and worked regularly each day. He was bridled for the first time, then put into a harness to be trained for gaits and to teach him basic commands. Work in the harness with a light training cart helped steady him, set his head, and accustom him to the feel of leather on his body and trailing lines around his legs. As Storm progressed in each step of his schooling, the señor took heart. He began to feel confident that he would have no trouble winning the race and the bet. Storm's temperament seemed good, though he was full of fire. His intelligence helped him quickly learn and understand what these strange two-legged creatures wanted from him.

In the middle of summer, he was turned out to pasture again to run and strengthen his muscles. He had grown in height and stood at fourteen hands. His legs had lengthened; his muscles were getting more powerful each day from the steady work and exercise. He gave promise of being a big, strong horse; perhaps even bigger than his mighty sire.

Again winter arrived in the valley. The subdued excitement stirred amongst the people as spring approached. This year, Storm would be a two-year-old, eligible for the championship race in Chihuahua. This race had been run every year for seventy-five years. Only the very best horses could hope to win, and Mexico was becoming known for its fine horse-flesh. Everyone dreamt of winning the race, for the winner received $100,000 in gold, along with the coveted silver cup. The prestige of winning the race was highly prized by the owners, it brought buyers from far and near who hoped to purchase a colt or filly from the breeder of the winner. The top six horses were then eligible to run in the great stake race for four-year-olds that was also held at Chihuahua. At four years, the horses were at full growth. This stake race demanded every bit of speed, strength, heart, and courage that a horse possessed. It was a course of five miles and had been set up to test the horses for just such things. In the last three years, señor Gomez' stallions had won the two-year-old race and the four-year-old stake race. The winner of the stake race was assured a high breeder's fee for his stallion. Owners from as far as Europe brought their mares to these winners for breeding. The stud fees for these stallions were fantastically high, with only the very best mares accepted.

Spring approached and Storm's training excelled; he was carrying a light rider and working out on the homemade track on the ranchero. Excitement mounted as the people watched this tremendous young stallion run. He was a thing of power and beauty to behold. Storm was almost fifteen hands in height; his muscles had developed immensely in the last year. His temperament showed none of the traits of his desert ancestors and the señor began to believe that his colour meant good luck instead of bad, for Storm could run! His running was limited to short bursts now as his training was concentrated on building wind and muscle. The race was a mile and a half and Storm would be ready. Once in a while, Storm wouldn't let his jockey hold him; he would open up for a time before his rider could bring him back under control. Events like this showed that Storm had speed to burn. His hooves thundered on the hard-packed track like rolling army kettle drums. The wind whistled about his rider's ears and brought tears to his eyes. The colt looked like a whirling ball of fire storming around the track.

The people began to call him Firestorm and looked at him with pride; this tremendous young son of El Baroun. They believed he would clean up at the upcoming race when they placed their wagers. It would make up for the past three years when they had gone down in defeat. The favourite to win again this year was señor Gomez's stallion, Diablo.

The time for the race drew near; the date was set for June 21, the Feast of the Sacred Heart.

CHAPTER III
The Loss of the Legend

Spring blossomed in the valley. Storm was progressing rapidly and his fast workouts had stepped up. It was a week before the race and everyone was getting ready to start the journey to Chihuahua. They would travel for three days with one day of rest before Storm partook in the big race. The weather had been lovely so far, but now storm clouds loomed over the Sierra Madres. The peons and vaqueros looked anxiously at the clouds as a bad storm would make it hard to travel to Chihuahua. Such harsh weather would take more out of Storm than if the weather should stay balmy.

They lit candles in the small chapel, but to no avail; the storm clouds kept building and were soon rolling into the valley. The wind sprang up and the timber began to bend as the storm gained in volume and intensity.

The rain came and with it hail. Hail the size of the señor's oranges. It lashed at the valley. Everything in sight scurried to find shelter from this falling white death. In no time the orchards were stripped, the grass was pounded flat, and the garden ruined. The crops of maize were flattened as if some giant roller had run over them. Windows smashed in the hacienda. Everyone hurried, placing the animals in the stable for protection while covering items around the house. Señor moved quickly, placing Storm in the stall himself.

In the stable the storm was muted, but still terrible in its ferocity. The horses were restless in their stalls. It was as if an angry god was exacting penance from this valley for some misdeed. Storm paced his stall. He hated the confinement of it, wanting to be out so he could tackle the storm; a similar storm in which he had been born into. He was not afraid of it, he felt some strange kinship with this wild outpouring of the heavens.

A hailstone crashed in his window. It startled him, sending him against the door of his stall. The sudden weight on the door caused it to crack and shudder. Storm pawed angrily at it. He wanted out. He struck again. The door gave, swinging outward. He charged through and out the far open doors of the stable. He would meet the storm on his own terms with no confining walls to hold him.

Once outside, the full fury of the storm hit him. He reared to meet it. A hailstone gave him a stunning blow on his head. Then another, and another pelted down on him. He had indeed taken on a worthy adversary, for there was no fighting this thing. He took to his heels, every instinct telling him to make for the high timber and shelter in the cloud-shrouded mountains.

Faster and faster he went, with the storm pushing him forward. Hail still barraged him. He was cut and bleeding in a dozen places. He forged ahead, his strong young muscles enabling him to pull ahead of the storm, outrunning it. Soon he was in the foothills of the vast Sierra Madres. His speed slowed, but he continued on, moving before the storm. The rain and hail obliterated his tracks.

He travelled all night. By morning he was high in the mountains, following an old Indigenous trail that led to the summit. It dropped down on the other side towards the harsh desert. Here no man ventured. Few animals found it habitable except rattlesnakes and Gila monsters. It took two weeks for Storm to traverse the mountains. He moved steadily, stopping only for necessary food and water before continuing on. His instinct was sending him to the kind of home his ancestors had known generations before him. His lungs expanded as he breathed deeply at the high altitude. Previously unused muscles appeared and were developed in the strenuous climb of the massive slopes of the Madres.

Storm moved onward; he never hesitated or looked back. He did not think of the ranchero or of the señor and the people. He was looking continually ahead to where his instinct impelled him. He gloried in his newfound freedom. He was confident in himself and his ability to handle anything that might lie before him, for in him coursed the blood of his ancestors. It urged him to make his own way in the harsh and bitter desert that called him ever on.

Back at the ranchero, the storm vented its fury all night and no one stirred. The señor slept, content in the knowledge that all was well. With the morning the sun would shine and shine it did. Everything seemed so peaceful. The señor got ready to go to the stables to check on his horses. Before he left the house, his foreman's son came running into the hacienda, out of breath from his exertion. He blurted out that Storm was gone.

"Of course the storm is gone, my young friend," replied the señor, laughing at the boy's breathlessness.

"No, no, señor. Storm is gone. Our Storm, the colt. He is gone, señor!" Juan cried.

"What … but this cannot be, I put him into his stall myself when the storm hit," the señor said.

"His door is broken. He is gone, señor," Juan replied.

"Quickly, go get the men," commanded the señor. "We must go after him immediately. In his fear of the storm, he will have travelled far and fast, and may have hurt himself in the dark."

The vaqueros were soon mounted and waiting in the court-yard of the hacienda. The señor was riding El Baroun. The men were mounted on the señor's Arabians for they would have to travel fast to find the young Storm. They carried food and blankets in case an overnight camp was necessary. They started out, and when they reached the middle of the valley the señor called a halt. He consulted with his men as to which direction they should go in search of the colt. The men had realized that all hope of tracking him was lost because of the storm. They decided that the colt would have fled in front of the storm, and would have headed for the foothills to find shelter. Once they agreed upon this, they set out at a ground-covering pace. It was early in the afternoon when they reached the foothills. Above them towered the stately mountains. The señor and his men were at a loss as to where the colt might have gone. They discarded the idea that the young horse would have gone further up the mountains. They agreed that a sheltered horse such as the young Storm would stick to the foothills, so they decided to split into two groups. One to go south and the other north to see if they could pick up the colt's tracks. The two parties swung out in opposite directions, holding their horses to a fast, ground-covering lope. The señor said they would meet at their original spot in three days whether or not they had found any signs of the young stallion.

They camped out that night, far from the señor's ranchero. They rose with the first light of dawn and continued the search. Around every bend, the men hoped to catch sight of the young colt. Surely, he could not have travelled much farther. Usually, a loose horse will wander aimlessly, grazing along the way. Only a horse that knows where it is going will keep moving steadily when free. As the men knew this, they kept expecting to catch up with Storm at any moment. Or else, they reasoned, the other party might have already done so. Each group of searchers continued. Each one's hope of finding the colt diminishing with each passing hour and its many miles.

At this time, Storm was climbing higher up the mountains with no thought except the growing urge to reach the place calling to him.

That evening the vaqueros camped 150 miles from home. Their horses were beginning to show signs of wear. In the morning, the two groups would head back to their meeting place, each confident that the other had found the colt.

Arriving back at their starting point, the men glanced at one another with stunned looks of disbelief. The señor seemed ill. An uncomfortable silence surrounded them. They loosened cinches and averted their eyes from the disappointment expressed on señor Delgado's face. They pondered where the colt could be. After all, they could have passed within two miles of him and not known, or he could have been up any one of the thousand canyons or draws. They had seen no tracks. The señor finally ordered his men to remount. They returned to the ranchero with a growing fear nagging them. Perhaps they would not be able to recover Storm in time for the big race. The señor sent his men to all the nearby ranches, telling his friends to keep a lookout for his colt. His prize colt. His winner of races to be. His blood bay colt; the colt with the colour of living fire. This throwback to those fierce desert stallions of long ago.

By this time, Storm had reached the summit of the pass and was travelling down the mountains. He knew that whatever was pulling him was down there.

No word was sent to the señor that his colt had been sighted. As the days passed without word, the señor seemed to age overnight. All of his hopes and dreams slowly fell away. On the morning of the fifth day, señor Gomez and some of his men again paid a visit to señor Delgado. At first, señor Delgado's hopes rose when he saw them ride in, but this quickly passed when Pedro Gomez greeted him.

"So, you have lost your miracle colt, I hear," he said with a rather pleased look on his face. "Or have you decided that he is not good enough to run against my black Diablo?"

"My colt would have outrun your Diablo so badly that you would not have believed it, even though you saw it!" replied the señor, angrily.

"Ho, so you think, but if he must default, how can he win?" asked Gomez. "He will surely default if you do not find him within the next few days, for the race is but nine days away, my friend."

"And you will still hold me to that foolish bet?" asked the señor.

"But of course, unless your word is as worthless to others as this colt seems to be to you!" Pedro replied.

"My word is good," stated the señor coldly, "and if the colt does not return in time for the race, the terms of the bet will be paid in full."

"Good," replied Pedro Gomez. "I shall return home then, hoping that I will hear more news of this fabulous colt with the colour of fire. Firestorm is what he is called by the peons."

"If the colt does not return in time, I suppose you will let me keep him to glory in his absence?" the señor asked sarcastically.

"Of course you may keep him. What would I want with a phantom horse, one that is already dead at the fangs of a mountain lion?" replied Gomez, laughing. "You may keep your lost colt and dream of him often in the absence of all your others. I will return after the race to claim by bet!"

An air of sadness descended over the hacienda in the days that followed. It affected everyone from the señor down to the lowliest stable boy. Storm did not return. The morning of the race dawned clear and fine, but the atmosphere at the ranchero was undisturbed in its melancholy. A week after the race, señor Gomez and his top vaqueros again rode into the courtyard of the hacienda. Señor Delgado went to meet him with the broken walk of a man many years his senior.

"You have come to collect your bet, I see," he said.

"Yes, I told you I would be back. Today I feel on top of the world. My colt, Diablo, won the two-year-old championship by ten lengths! In my happiness, I have decided to go easy on you, my friend. You may keep your ranchero, your cattle, and your sheep. But your Arabians I will have, down to the last newborn foal. All except your missing colt. I don't want a throwback, such as he, to mingle his blood with my horses."

The señor nodded his head brokenly. He could not bring himself to beg this man for anything. Not even his gentle

Surur. So his prized band was brought forward, one by one, and were roped together in a long line to be led away by the vaqueros. Last of all Surur, was tied to the foreman's saddle and then the mighty El Baroun was brought forward. Señor Gomez decided that he would ride this great stallion himself, leading mare Surur. He mounted and looked down at señor Delgado, saying, "Never fear, I will take good care of them. They will make me famous. Now my horses will be in demand all over the world. When Diablo wins the four-year-old stake race in two years' time, there will be no end to where my Arabians and I will go!"

The señor watched the procession until long after they were gone from sight. He then turned and went back into the hacienda, an old and heartbroken man.

CHAPTER IV
The Desert Legend

Storm was still enjoying his newfound freedom. He had descended the other side of the mountain where the air was dryer and hotter. He made his way out of the foothills to the edge of the desert, and it was here where the pull had drawn him. The smell of the hot and burning sand assailed his nostrils, filling him with a desire to explore further. This was a land of limitless waste and sand. Here and there large cacti raised their thorny spines. Tumbleweeds drifted aimlessly, jostled by the slight breeze. Buzzards floated effortlessly across the pale blue sky, searching for something or someone that had pitted itself against this harsh land and lost. Rattlesnakes sunned themselves lazily in hidden places, daring anyone to disturb their solitude. Gila monsters darted over the broken surface of the shifting sands, intent, it seemed, upon some important business.

Storm's nostrils flared, taking in all the smells. His ears were pointed forward to catch the slightest sound in this quiet wasteland. He started forward. His hooves sank into the soft sand as he made his way into the burning furnace. He never hesitated, striking out in a straight line towards the far horizon.

He travelled at a steady pace, conserving his energy. He went further and further, the miles of sand falling behind him. The cacti grew thinner and farther apart. He pushed steadily ahead, once shifting his direction only slightly to the left. Night found him still travelling, his pace still steady and purposeful. He climbed a sand dune and before him laid his destination.

The oasis was a mile wide and extended for two miles in length. The smell of water reached him. He quickened his stride. He left the desert with the sure instinct of his forebears. He seemed to know that such a haven would always be found in this harsh land. On the edge of the oasis, he reached the spring. It seeped from an underground river that formed a large pool, which was shaded by trees and willows. He drank long and deep. Walking ahead, with all his senses alert, he made for the highest point to look over his new domain. Nothing stirred. The oasis was bathed in the pale glow of moonlight. Storm listened and smelled. He heard a brush rabbit scurrying through the sage underbrush. An owl hooted nearby. The coyotes started their song; a song they send each evening to the shining moon. Storm listened and waited. The sounds he strove to hear were not forthcoming. Finally satisfied that all was at peace, he started grazing on the harsh grass that grew by the spring. Morning found him resting beneath the shade of the trees. Soon he would graze often in order to regain his strength from his vigorous trek over the mountains and through the desert.

For the next six months, Storm stayed in his hideaway, exploring his island home. On fine mornings, he lowered his head and bucked. He raced around his paradise with the high spirits of a vigorous, growing youngster. One morning while grazing, Storm lifted his head to test the wind. His flaring nostrils smelled the hot burning sand that surrounded his island home. Instinct warned him that all was not right. The sun was getting hazy and the wind was starting to hum with a persistent whine. Storm watched the birds flying rapidly into the trees, seeking shelter from some unseen menace. The trees started to sway in the rising wind. The smell of burning sand was getting stronger in the air. Storm pawed restlessly and began to trot in ever-widening circles. He sensed some impending danger—he could smell it—as it hovered menacingly in the air. He neighed his challenge into the teeth of the wind and the growing crescendo answered him. The sun was hidden. Out on the desert the sand was whirling in high-rising swirls. Storm moved ahead, seeking the protection of the spring with its thick stand of trees and matted willows. He plunged into the middle of them, turning to face the approaching wall of sand that was coming at the oasis with the speed of a locomotive. The sandstorm hit with the suddenness of a charging rhinoceros and with a like force. The driving sand blotted out the sun. The grains of sand stung every living thing like a hive of angry hornets; it filled the animal's ears, eyes, fur, and feathers, making breathing an almost impossible task. It smothered everything. It tore at the breath, screaming like thousands of banshees. The sand filled the pool and covered the grass, the sagebrush, and all but buried the trees and shrubs. There was no escape from its choking fury.

Storm turned his back to the wind, lowered his head, shut his eyes, and partially closed his nostrils to the howling death. The sandstorm whirled over and around him. He felt like hours had passed, but it was only a matter of minutes before the fury of the wind had died. All became quiet on the once beautiful oasis, but it was no longer a garden of Eden: the sand had reclaimed the island. Now it looked similar to the rest of the desert, except for the odd tree sticking incongruously out of the piles of sand. Storm looked around him and shook the sand from his body, pawing at the covered spring. Then, without another backward glance, he set out across the burning wastes towards the foothills from which he had come.

He travelled steadily. Storm was two and a half years old. For some time, he had been missing the company of his own kind. He had grown considerably during the last six months. His muscles had filled out and had strengthened. He was approaching the prime of his life. His blood was coursing fast with vigour. He had confidence in his ability and was ready to take on all comers. Storm soon reached the foothills of the mountains the following day. His island oasis behind him but, in time, the winds would blow the sand away and it would bloom again. It was always there, waiting. Storm knew this surely; it was the knowledge inherited from his desert forebears.

When he reached the foothills, he headed north along the foot of the mountains. He found water and grazed as he moved. Every once in a while he stopped, sending his challenging neigh reverberating through the hills. He would fling up his head and run, just for the sheer love of running, often moving up and down the hills and onto the sandy desert floor. Sometimes he would forge higher into the mountains to investigate some strange smell that was brought to him on the wind. He moved slowly but surely northward along the foothills of the Sierra Madres. He began to encounter the odd flock of sheep and scattered herds of grazing cattle. A few hardy ranches were situated amongst these hills, canyons, and draws at the base of the mountains.

Storm quickened his pace. He was alert and watchful, continually testing the wind to read the news it would bring to him. He turned inward towards the mountains and came out on a high plateau, surveying the valley that stretched below him. Far to the north, his eyes caught the movement of a band of horses. Their dust drifted skyward as they moved. Storm neighed after them, then whirled, making his way down the steep rocky slopes to the floor of the valley in swift pursuit. He ran as surefooted as a mountain goat and raced after the band, sending his ringing challenge towards them, and swiftly began to close the gap.

The band ceased to move forward and began to mill in a circle, turning to face this fast- approaching horse. A big ugly brute of a horse separated himself from the band of milling horses, coming forward to meet this intruder. He was the herd stallion, supreme lord over the band of mares and foals in his care. He sounded a challenge to Storm, warning him to come no closer. His instinct told him that there would be a dangerous rival to his kingship.

Storm stopped twenty feet away. He did not want to fight. In him was a growing desire to force his way past this barrier to get to the exciting smells and sounds of these strange horses. He pawed the ground, trying to go around the herd sire to reach the band that was frozen in a circle of imaginary but restrictive bounds. They watched with ears pricked; their curiosity about this newcomer showed in their eyes.

The herd stallion trumpeted another warning, then charged straight towards Storm. At the last second, before colliding with the young stallion, he whirled and lashed at Storm with both hind feet. Storm swerved aside but the hooves caught him a glancing blow on his shoulder. Its force sent him rolling.

Storm regained his footing and turned to face the stallion. He was getting angry. The desire to fight this enemy was rising within him; this enemy keeping him from the mares. The stallion eyed Storm warily. He had hoped that the first attack would have been enough to frighten the young stallion off, but Storm showed no signs of fear. The old stallion was well past his prime. He had been in many battles with younger stallions who tried to challenge his leadership. His grey coat was shaggy and battle-scarred. He would fight to the death to protect his band. There could be only one herd stallion.

He charged again, but this time Storm was ready and charged to meet him. They rose high, pawing and striking at each other. Each trying to pound the other to the ground. They broke apart and whirled to eye each other. Then, as if on some unheard signal, they charged again; this time passing by each other while trying to land a killing blow on one another's backs. They whirled to meet again, seeking to tear out each other's jugulars with their teeth. They screamed their fury and the echoes of their furious charges resounded through the hills.

Storm's strength and endurance were taking their toll on the older horse. He was cut and bleeding in a dozen places, but still fresh. The old grey-faced Storm, waiting for the next charge. His sides were covered with foam and he knew that the next charge would decide his fate.

Storm screamed again. Now all the fighting blood of his fierce desert ancestors was coming to the fore. His brain cleared as an onrush of cold fury possessed him. He went forward to meet his adversary again with all the inborn cunning of his heritage. He suddenly charged. This time, instead of going past, he swerved and shook his head won like a rattler, seizing the right foreleg of the grey in his jaws and snapping the old stallion's cannon bone with ease.

When the grey turned to face Storm, he stood on three legs. He knew that the next charge would be his last. He expected no mercy, for he would have given none. This was the law of nature—only the fittest and strongest should survive.

Storm neighed his challenge then quickly charged, for he too sensed that victory was his. He hit the grey with all the power of his young bone and muscle, knocking the herd leader off his feet. Storm reared and came down with pounding front feet. They struck blows like a wielded sledgehammer. The grey lay still. Storm pawed the ground. Lifting his head, he flung his ringing neigh of victory into the wind so all could hear and take notice.

He then turned to the mares. They came forward to greet him, their jealously reared as they kicked and squealed with excitement when trying to be near him. Storm nipped and bit playfully, rising pride and excitement stirring in him as he realized this band was now his to look after, down to the last little foal. Then Storm started to nip in earnest, exerting his will over the mares. It was necessary that they learn to obey his slightest command. Faster and faster he proceeded to round them up and get them moving before him. One reluctant mare tried to slip away and was reprimanded by Storm. This showed her it would be best to obey her new leader. She fell into line, then forged ahead to the front of the band. Storm had them moving in full flight. He guided them northward, aiming them towards the mountains to the more concealed draws and canyons hidden in their vastness.

They spent the next three months grazing along the mountainside, sometimes going out of the foothills to race along the desert edge in the wild, feeling an outpouring of joy in their freedom. This band was not like Storm. They were wild mustangs who had roamed the vast Sierra Madres for years. They were small, mixed horses of different breeding. They were tough animals, capable of travelling far and fast on very poor food. Storm was quickly learning the duties of being a leader. He found the best grass for his band and led them to clear springs of cold mountain water. He stood guard so that the prowling wolves and mountain lions could not sneak up on his grazing band; he was kept on constant alert. His senses sharpened and his muscles hardened from the constant move- ment of going up and down the mountainsides and from his runs on the sandy desert. He was approaching his third year. He was young and had much to learn about the ways of the world. For now, he was content with his life, taking glory in his strength, in his confidence, and in his ability to cope with anything that threatened his band.

Following the chain of the mountains, not caring where they went, they steadily moved northward; sometimes being pushed by the storms that came out of the mountains. Sometimes, in the far distance, they saw men on horseback. When this happened, the mares became nervous and fled in a wild stampede that Storm could not stop. He did not share their fear of these men. It did not matter, though a good run was something he was always enjoyed. He would catch his band and forge to the front, leading them for miles in a wild stampede up and down hills, canyons, and draws. Over the roughest terrain, he learned to race with the surefootedness of a mountain horse. When the band finally slowed, Storm was still fresh, looking like he had been on a jaunt when he had just covered five or six miles.

The weeks passed and Storm and his band still grazed northward, living the free life of wild horses.

CHAPTER V
Concerning other Forces in the Legend

Across the mountains, far to the south, time seemed to pass slowly at the hacienda. The peons on the ranchero were troubled by the loss of the colt and what it meant to their señor. He was taking less and less interest in his ranch. He was withdrawn and never discussed his foolish bet or the loss of his Arabians. Things were not faring well with the ranchero's business. The people were a humble lot, but were only too willing to believe that with the loss of Storm their luck had changed. They did not work as diligently as they had before. As a result, the cattle and sheep were not flourishing as they once had. Bad luck seemed to dog them. The cattle stampeded during a storm and dozens were killed. The sheep came down with a strange disease and hundreds died before it ran its course. The grass seemed sparser. The rains that always came did not come that year. The stable became decrepit from disuse. The once gleaming windows were caked with dirt and the stalls were full of old, dusty hay. A few chickens scratched aimlessly around it. Mice scurried to and from, finding a haven in this deserted place. The fruit in the orchards were left to ripen, falling to the ground, with the undergrowth already making inroads. The gardens were choked with weeds. The courtyard of the hacienda, which once had bloomed with flowers, now looked drab and lifeless.

The señor constantly thought of Surur, bitterly blaming himself for having lost her. It had been an act of nature that had lost him this colt, but the loss of Surur and El Baroun was brought about by his foolish pride. He came to believe that the colour of the blood bay colt had indeed been a bad omen. A sign of what was to come. Some days he would walk into the valley and stand gazing towards the summit of the mountains. He wondered about his colt and if he were still alive.

It had been almost a year since Storm had disappeared. The señor had given up hope of the colt returning on his own. He felt that Storm must be dead, killed by some stalking mountain lion or from a fall over some precipice. He knew that a colt like his, raised and pampered in his first two years, would be ill-equipped to stand up to the rigors of life in the wild. He had forgotten the times when he had expounded his theories of why the Arabian was the best breed of horses in the world. In his depression, he seemed to forget his knowledge of the breed. Their intelligence. Their strength and staying power. Their great hearts and courage.

The months slowly passed, each day stretching endlessly into the next. The señor and his people moved listlessly about their work. One day, the señor was surprised to see Pedro Gomez ride into the ranch. He had not seen Gomez since the day his rival had taken the señor's Arabians. Señor Gomez looked around him at the neglect. He felt the hopelessness in the air of this once happy and prosperous ranchero. He noticed how the señor moved slowly towards him and felt a momentary pang of conscience over the bet that had cost Delgado so dearly.

"Well, Gomez, what can I do for you today?" asked the señor. "I suppose you have come to collect the rest of our bet now."

Señor Gomez flushed and began to speak, but then stopped. "No," he said, "I only came to tell you that your horses are being well looked after. Surur is due to foal again. I thought you would like to know how she is."

"Thank you for coming then. Will the sire of her new colt be your big black stallion, El Dorado?" he asked.

"No, I decided to breed her back to your El Baroun after all. Though I hope I will not get another colt like her last!" he replied. "That colt of yours was no good, a throwback to those fierce desert horses of long ago. Else he would not have strayed far the night of the storm and would have been easy to find the next day."

"Perhaps you are right. In fact, I believe you are absolutely right. Yet… sometimes I wake from a dream in which I see him running. In this dream, he runs with unbelievable speed. He moves so fast that his body seems to burn with a living fire. His black mane and tail streaming in the wind. I know then that he is alive, somewhere, and running. Then I wake and realize it is only a dream. But for a while hope abounds in me that he will come back. Then, my friend, we would see a horse that we have never seen before." the señor mused.

"I don't believe there is a horse alive that could compare with my black colt, Diablo. There is a horse, I tell you. When he matures another year, he will win the four-year-old race at

Chihuahua. He will be the most sought-after sire on this continent." Gomez stated emphatically.

"So you think, but if Storm were to run against him, a different story would be told. Storm's bloodlines are better than that of your black colt," the señor replied.

"I disagree with you on that," Gomez said laughing, "but I tell you what… if your colt, by some miracle, manages to beat my black Diablo, I will return all of your Arabians to you, including all the new foals that will be born in the meantime. How is that for a bet? If you can believe in all those miracles!" he added.

"It is a bet, though they say the age of miracles is long past," said señor Delgado. "If he should return, a whole year has been lost in his training, you know."

"True, true, but surely such a miracle horse would need no training, eh, my friend?" Gomez jokingly replied.

He turned his horse and called back to the señor, saying that he hoped to see him at the race in Chihuahua, along with his lost colt. Then he departed, laughing.

While señor Delgado and señor Gomez spoke, across the mountains far to the north—in the land of the Gringo's—sat two cowboys who were hunched over their campfire in the brushland of southwest Texas. Jed Owens and Bill Dunbar had returned to their ranch after the war between the states to find all their cattle running wild in the brush. Their ranch had fallen into complete disrepair and there was no cash available to start rebuilding. Over coffee, they sat and talked about ways they could make cash to help get themselves back into the cattle business.

Jed emptied the coffee pot, looked up at Bill and said, "I wonder if we could catch some wild horses and sell them to the other ranchers?"

"That's a good idea," replied Bill. "The ranchers will be needing extra horses for their remudas if they decide to make the long drive to Kansas City with their herds."

"We'll have to start soon if we want to catch enough and have them partially broke by the fall round up or by next spring," said Jed.

"I'll ride into town to get our supplies for the trip," said Bill. "I'll meet you back here in two days."

"Good enough," replied Jed. "While you're gone, I'll round up a couple of pack horses and some extra fast saddle horses for us. We'll need them to relay the wild horses."

When Bill returned with their supplies, the two friends made ready for the long trip to the country of wild horses. They decided to swing down into Mexico to the Sierra Madre range as many bands of wild horses roamed the foothills of these mountains. It would take them two weeks of hard riding to reach a place to set up camp.

Months of hard work and harder riding were ahead of them. Once a band was located, the men would follow them, learning their habits and where they most often strayed. The band's water holes would be sought out and once found, a trap would be built at one. Then would come the days of long hours in the saddle. They would keep hazing the horses, never letting them rest and never letting them get enough to eat or drink. Finally, the band would approach their hidden trap. The herd would be tired and thirsty and the cowboys would be able to close in on them. After the horses were captured, the men would begin breaking the pick of the bunch. This would take weeks of back-breaking, bone-jarring work.

Bill and Jed led two extra saddle horses and a pack mule. They were carrying enough supplies for a three-month trip. They would supplement their grub with whatever game they managed to shoot along the way. A week later saw them growing beards, already travel-worn as they crossed the border between the States and Mexico. They had ridden 300 miles in seven days. They stopped at a small village fifty miles into Mexico to get the pack mule shoed in preparation for the long trip still ahead of them.

They started early on the ninth day after spending the night in the Mexican village; much refreshed after sleeping in a real bed and having a bath. A week later they were moving steadily across the desert lands of Mexico, with the foothills of the Madres visible on the horizon. Another five days and they reached the foothills with weary horses and were almost exhausted themselves. Though they knew where the water holes were located, the trek across the desert had taken its toll.

Bill and Jed decided to stop and let their horses recuperate. In the shape they were in, they would not be able to keep up with the relentless work of pushing a wild herd of horses. They set up camp in the foothills and laid their plans for the capture of a least thirty wild horses.

Unknowingly, a hundred miles to the south, Storm and his band were moving forward to a meeting predestined by fate.

CHAPTER VI
The Capture of the Legend

Storm lifted his head to smell the morning breeze that blew in from the north. He had grown during the last six months and was close to sixteen hands. He had filled out a great deal. His muscles rippled and flowed under silken skin when he moved. Running with the wild ones had toughened his muscles, turning them to iron. He was fast approaching full maturity. His development quickened by the life he had led for the past year. The constant movement of the band, stampeding up and down steep slopes, had built his staying power. He paused again to test the wind. During the last few days, he had caught glimpses of a man on horseback behind him.

He was looking at his grazing band grazing below him when a man burst from cover to the side of them, whirling his lariat. The startled band leaped away and with Storm's loud neigh ringing in their ears, they flew towards the mountain stronghold. Storm plunged down the hill overtaking them, racing to the front. He led them away from the human menace who soon became part of the distance behind them. They ran for miles, up hills and down, over ravines, and through the sparsely wooded lower reaches of the mountains. Finally, they slowed and started to graze, but another man appeared from nowhere and they ran away from him in a mad dash. This time they did not run as far. They were nervous and only snatched mouthfuls of grass as they moved towards a water hole. The lead mare approached the water hole at sunset that first day. As she drew near, a man on horseback came out of the brush. The herd stampeded once again. They ran as hard and as long as they could. When night fell, they were trying to graze restlessly. They moved steadily towards another watering hole deeper in the hills.

Bill and Jed had crossed the band's trail after three weeks of searching. They had rested their horses a week at their first camp. For another two weeks they kept an eye on the herd, only following them until the men learned the bands watering holes and habits. Now they had started to drive the herd. They would keep after them day and night, never letting them graze or drink from the watering holes. The men's horses were well-rested. They drove the herd continually. From early morning until late at night they kept the wild bunch moving steadily.

The band was tiring. After three days of running, with very little grazing and water, they were gradually slowing down. They did not stampede so frantically when the men moved upon them. During mid-morning of the fourth day, Storm led a weary band to a water hole in the canyon at the far end of a small valley. The nervous tensions were wearing off Storm now, the band was too tired, hungry, and thirsty to be alert. They approached the water hole slowly, but the smell of the cool freshwater drove all fear from their minds. They ran forward to drink, and this time the men did not frighten them away.

When they had drunk their fill, they started to graze eagerly at the abundant grass growing near the spring. Storm suddenly raised his head and his nostrils flared as he caught the scent of the men who had been hounding them for days. He sent out a ringing command and headed the band at a fast run for the entrance to the canyon. When they got there, the way out was barred by a solid wall of brush and poles. The band whirled away as they sought a way out of the valley, but there was no way out. The canyon walls rose sharply on each side and the only entrance was blocked. Soon they settled down to graze. Water was near and the grass was plentiful.

Bill and Jed set up camp at the entrance to the valley canyon. They were pleased with their work. They would start cutting out all the young stallions and fillies from the main band tomorrow and let the rest go. They wanted young stuff: two, three, and four-year-olds. They talked about their plans far into the night.

"I figure we should be able to handle twenty to thirty head, don't you, Jed?" said Bill.

"Yeah, between the two of us, we ought to get their rough edges off and start for home in a month," replied Jed.

"What do you think of that stallion?" Bill asked.

"He's some horse!" replied Jed. "He's got me stumped as to what he's doing out here though."

"What do you mean?" asked Bill.

"Well, the way I see it, that's no ordinary bronc. He's nothing like the rest of this band. Did you notice how he can run? He reminds me of a picture I saw one time during the war. We were in General Lee's quarters and he had this picture of a horse. It was a big grey stallion. There was something about the head of that horse that reminds me of this wild stud. I think the General said it was a picture of a purebred Arabian," mused Jed.

"What would a purebred Arabian be doing in this God-forsaken country?" asked Bill.

"That's what's got me stumped, but if we can get a rope on that horse and break him to the saddle, we might get a bigger price for him than all the rest of these mustangs put together," stated Jed.

"Well, we'd best turn in, it's an early rise in the morning. There's lots to be done in the next month if we want to be back home before fall round up." Bill said.

At the break of dawn, Jed and Bill saddled their cow horses and proceeded to round up Storm's band. They cut out all the mares with foals at foot, hazing them away from the rest of the band. Jed herded them to one side of their brush barricade while Bill proceeded to cut an opening in it. The two cowboys chased the mares and foals through this, then reclosed it.

They had pushed Storm, the young fillies, two-year-old stallions, and dry mares to the other end of the valley after splitting the band. This weeding took the men a full day, with barely a pause for the noonday meal. The next day, Jed and Bill were up at the crack of dawn to build a corral to use for rough breaking. They roped the horses one by one and pulled them into the corral. One horse would be tied securely to the snubbing post in the center. It was here that the tough, heart-breaking, and bone-jarring work of the two cowboys began. There was no time for the gentleness and patience that Storm had received in his early years.

The young horses were brought in shaking and filled with terror. They were tied tight with a saddle cinched on. A war bridle was fashioned on each as the men proceeded to take turns bucking them out. The horses reared, bucked, sun-fished, and twisted. They grunted their pain and fear. They fought until they were exhausted and stood with their heads and tails low. These proud, high-spirited creatures were brought from the heights of freedom to the lowliness of servitude. Some would never regain their fierce, proud ways. They were broken in spirit. Like an animated doll: workable but lifeless. The joy in living was gone. Some were born as outlaws, though. They were tripped out until they could no longer fight, but they could never be trusted. They were innately vicious and though a horse that was born an outlaw is rare, he is usually made that way from the abuse of men.

The men kept at this for three solid weeks, sometimes breaking out as many as two a day. The dry mares, two-year-old stallions, and the two, three, and four-year-old fillies that were roughed out were then put into another makeshift corral. As the days passed, Storm became more and more nervous. Every day two more of his band was rounded up, roped, and the rough edges of their spirits were worn down and broken. At the end of three weeks, Jed and Bill held a conference at their late scratch supper.

They were grubby and worn. Their eyes were red from lack of sleep and their muscles ached from the trials with the mustangs. Though tired, they were well satisfied knowing that forty-five horses of fair caliber were ready for the long trail back to Texas.

"I think we ought to nab that stud tomorrow and let the rest go, eh, Jed?" asked Bill.

"Yeah, but we ought to try roping him. For one thing, our horses aren't fast enough to put us within roping distance, and for another, I've got the feeling that he was handled by men somewhere. He doesn't run away with the same fear as the others. More like it's a game with him to outrun us," replied Jed.

"How do you think we should catch him then?" asked Bill.

"I don't know for sure," said Jed, "but I think we should try hazing him into the corral real slow. I have a feeling that once he's closed in and has a chance to calm down and look it over, he won't be much trouble. I'm willing to give it a couple more days anyhow. He ought to bring a price back home just on looks if nothing else."

"Okay by me," said Bill. "We'll try it your way in the morning."

The next morning, they opened the corral gate wide and made a long chute running up to the gate. Then they set out for the far end of the valley where Storm and the last few horses in the band habitually stayed. This time Jed and Bill circled wide, pushing the horses slowly towards the open end of the chute leading to the corral. Jed had tied up one of the quieter mares to the snubbing post and, with very little trouble, Storm and his remaining band were hazed inside. Jed and Bill then cut the rest of the band off from Storm and pushed them back out the chute, closing the corral gate behind them. Storm was trapped. He was a picture to behold. Racing around the corral with head and tail held high, he bugled his challenge for all to hear. He then stood quietly to await the coming events. Jed and Bill sat quietly on the top rail of the corral, watching him.

"Mark my words, Bill," said Jed, "the likes of that horse is something you won't ever see again. He's one in a million. Whoever owned that hoss must be sick at the loss of him. But there's no brand on him so we're free to claim him."

Storm's free life was over. A captive once more, he was back in the hands of man.

CHAPTER VII
The Captivity of the Legend

A month later, Jed and Bill hazed their band of mustangs towards Texas. They travelled slowly; it was no small feat for two men to run a group of half broke horses. Storm travelled with them. He wasn't running free anymore but roped and led by Jed.

It had taken only three days for Storm to accept his capture. From the moment that Jed approached him, memories of Storm's past flooded back into the Arabian's mind. He had been skittish and leery of being handled, but once he let Jed touch him, all of his forgotten training came back. He stood quietly. From there on it had been easy. They haltered him and led him around the corral, marvelling at his manners and docility. They moved slowly with him, neither one wanting to spoil this find. They decided to lead him home and sell him to someone who could break him properly with time and patience since their time was running out. On the fifth morning after Storm's capture, they tore down the brush barricade to the entrance of the canyon and headed northeast for Texas.

The leaves on the trees were starting to turn colour and the morning air had a decided nip to it when Jed and Bill finally reached their ranch. They arrived with Storm safely in tow, but the band of mustangs whittled down from forty-five to thirty. Seven had disappeared in a stampede crossing the desert. One had broken his leg in a badger hole and had to be put down. Three had died from drinking at a poisoned water hole and four of the worst outlaws had been turned loose.

They turned half-broken broncs into the corral by their ranch house. Storm was put into the one and only box stall in the barn. It was a far cry from the señor's magnificent stable. Here, the roof was low and the stable was dim, with light entering from two small windows and the open top half of the door. There was no packed clay on these floors, just old dirt covered with wisps of old straw. Storm did not like it. He pawed the floor, pacing the confines of his small prison. He was looking for a way out. This was not how he remembered things.

Jed and Bill left early the next day. They had decided to ride to the nearest and largest ranch to try and sell Storm and the rest of his band. They would ask $500 for Storm and thirty dollars apiece for the mustangs. With this cash, they could restock their ranch with cattle and repair their buildings and fences. It was twenty miles to their closest neighbour. It was a large ranch, one of the biggest in Texas and it covered some 400 square miles of the best cattle land in the West.

Jed and Bill rode into the main ranch yard a day later. They were shown into the large living room. Navajo rugs covered the floors and a big set of longhorns hung above the huge fireplace. They talked to the owner, Rex Barton, and explained the purpose of their visit. When they described Storm, Mr. Barton laughed and said, "I can tell you two are old horse traders. No horse could be as perfect as the one you're describing, especially some wild stud."

"Come see for yourself," said Jed.

"I think I will," said Mr. Barton. "I need those extra horses for my remuda. We're planning on having a cattle drive up over the Chisholm Trail to Kansas City next spring. I'd like to see this wonder horse for myself."

"When will you come?" Bill asked.

"I'll return with you tomorrow. My foreman and top wrangler will want to see the horses before I buy them," he replied.

Jed and Bill met Mr. Barton's top wrangler, Andy Dawson, later that day. When they talked to him about the red stallion they had picked up with the wild bunch, he too was skeptical of their stories. Andy Dawson was from the old school of horse breakers. He knew his business inside and out. In his training, there was little room for patience and gentle handling. He thought that horses were dumb beasts that had to be bent to his will. When he finished breaking a horse you could say it was well broke. It could turn on a dime and give you five cents change! It would chase out a thousand-pound steer from the main herd and bring its rider within roping distance fast. It could dump the steer quickly and hold it down, and it would neck rein beautifully. It would back straight and true. It would go from a standing start to a full gallop. But, it would be an *it*. There would be no joy in its working, no partnership with its rider, just servitude. It would work through fear: fear of the spur and fear of the whip. Such was the technique of Andy Dawson, and it was a standard of the times in Texas. Where a hundred horses were broken every spring, there was no time for patience and gentleness. This was the man Storm was soon to meet.

Three days later, Jed and Bill arrived back home accompanied by Mr. Barton and Andy Dawson. As they entered the old barn, Storm neighed his challenge and pawed the flooring of his stall. He made a perfect picture. Even the gloominess of the old barn could not detract from the red sheen of his body. His head was raised, his ears pricked and almost touching at the tips. His large fiery eyes burned with an inner glow that matched the outside flame of his coat. He stood looking at these men like a king surveying his new subjects. He was poised for instant action, ready to meet anything that might threaten his royal command.

Andy Dawson looked him over with the practiced eye of a knowing horseman. He noted the fine, broad forehead and the wide-set eyes, the nostrils that were large and flaring. His eye took in the clean line of the throat latch and supple neck. The long, sloping yet powerful shoulders. The deep, full chest and barrel. Room, and room to spare, for large lungs and a big heart. He noted the straight legs with the long tapering muscles well-tied into good solid bone. The perfect forty-five-degree angle of the sloping pasterns. He took in the short back, the strong, close coupled loins, and Storm's deep, full hindquarters. He saw a horse of near perfection, a horse that he had never laid eyes on in all of his days.

Storm did not like him. As Andy entered the stall, Storm neighed his challenge and Andy made his first mistake. He raised the whip he held in his right hand and struck his boot with a resounding smack, commanding the stallion in a harsh voice to, "Stand quiet!" before holding Storm's halter.

But this was no poorly bred mustang bronc that Andy was facing now. In Storm burned the spirit of royal Arabians, he did not back away or cringe. He pawed the ground and faced this human squarely. This man who dared to command.

Andy jerked the halter again, this time accompanying it instantly with a sharp flick of his whip on Storm's tender flank. Storm jumped ahead. He knew about whips. He had seen them used on rare occasions by the señor and his trainer on other colts they were breaking. It had never been necessary to use one on Storm. Once he understood what was expected of him, he willingly offered his obedience. The secret of Storm was to ask of him, not to demand.

As Storm plunged through the stall doorway, he brought Andy, still holding to the halter, along with him. When he regained his footing, Andy gave Storm another sharper flick of his whip even before he gave the command of, "Whoa."

Storm's nerves tightened up. He knew what was expected of him, but he needed the chance to give his cooperation before being forced. His heart smoldered and a tiny flame of resistance began to grow. He bided his time. Storm was not vicious. The señor had feared that this throwback would have the inborn viciousness of his cunning desert ancestors. It was not so, but he could not be taught to fear.

The days passed. Storm had been bought by Mr. Barton and taken to his ranch. Here Andy commenced to break him for use as a working stock horse, which Storm had all the necessary qualities. He could run at speed and slide to a complete and full stop. He could turn on a dime and he was smart, but he was given no chance to offer his willingness to perform.

Andy continued to make mistake after mistake with the stallion. He could not understand Storm's personality. He kept demanding instant obedience, first with the whip and then with the spur. This type of work was new to Storm. The bridle he wore now had a severe Spanish curb with a tight chain chin strap. When pulled back hard, it squeezed the bars of his lower jaw and hurt fearfully. The bit tore his tender mouth. The saddle born no resemblance to the light training and racing saddle he was used to: this was a heavyweight with big bucking rolls and long dangling stirrups. He did not like it. Andy wasted no time accustoming Storm to his new gear. He slapped the saddle on roughly and cinched it tight. Storm sidestepped and received a jerk from the bit that hurt his mouth. He was not asked to stand, he was punished before he knew what was expected of him.

During the next two months, Storm was worked day after day. He learned to cut a steer out of the herd and run it down. After Andy had roped it, he learned to put on the brakes and flip the steer, then hold the rope tight to keep it down. He was worked for long hours and the training was always the same. He obeyed through pain, not fear. He did not work willingly and there was no joy in his effort. The tiny flame of rebellion grew and seethed within his untamed heart.

He was used in the round up and the hard work put the finishing touches on his development. His muscles were like rippling, flexible bands of steel. He had not an ounce of superfluous fat on him. His coat shone a bright glossy red in the sun. He was in top condition. Andy thought he was progressing well. He did not look into Storm's eyes to notice the smoldering resentment they held.

Young Barry Stuart used to take time from his evening duties on the ranch to visit Storm's corral. He would watch the stallion pace restlessly. He sensed the anger and resentment burning in Storm and he understood. For all of his life, Barry had been ordered around. First by his rough and rowdy father and his three older brothers. His mother had died when he was eight-years-old, and it seemed that all the gentleness and kindness of life left with her. Barry's father started to drink heavily. In the next four years, Barry was boxed, pushed, bullied, and ordered about. When he was twelve, he ran away from home. He had come to the Barton ranch and had got a job doing the menial chores around the ranch yard. He had been here for two years, but he was also ordered about. He was never asked, he was told. In his heart burned a resentment of this kind of treatment too, and he understood how the big red stallion felt.

Every night for the past two months, Barry had gone down to the corral to see the huge stallion. He talked to him as he had never talked to any human. Storm would stop his pacing and stand with ears pricked listening to the gentle voice of the young boy. Between the two of them, a bond was forged. From Barry's need of a friend to love and from his understanding of Storm's temperament, the seed of love grew and strengthened as the weeks wore on.

Barry first attempted to handle Storm late one evening. He did so slowly and gently. He stretched out his hand and began to stroke Storm's beautiful silken neck. Storm turned his head and surrendered his heart. He shoved his head hard against Barry with a nicker of complete trust and contentment.

From then on there was no stopping them. Barry rode Storm in the moonlight. Long after the ranch was settled for the night, Barry would sneak out to Storm's corral. Storm would come eagerly forward with his nicker of greeting, and they would go out of the corral. Riding bareback, with no bridle or any kind needed, the two of them would race out onto the range, glorying in their freedom and each other's company. Barry seemed to become a living part of the giant stallion as they raced swiftly away. They would cut a steer from the herd and chase it eagerly, then herd it back into the main bunch. What joy, what fun! Here was how a horse was meant to work for man. Joyfully and willingly. Storm responded for Barry as he never would for Andy Dawson. Barry only had to ask and Storm gave his all from the deep well-spring of his mighty heart.

During the day, Andy's training of Storm continued and the young stallion's tiny flame of resentment was fanned into a glow. Barry noticed it one night when he approached Storm's corral. The big stallion did not settle down but kept pacing inside his corral. He kept one ear pricked towards the sound of Barry's voice. Stirring within him was the desire to get away, and with it was arising the homing instinct inherent in all animals. He did not belong here. His sixth sense was prodding him. He stopped pacing and faced southwest towards the direction from which the pull was coming. The call to the home of his birthplace. He pawed the ground restlessly and bugled his challenge to the world that kept him prisoner.

Barry approached him slowly. "What's the matter, big fella? Do you want out and away from here, boy? I guess having me just isn't enough, eh, fella?" Storm turned to look, nudging him hard with his nose. Then he turned towards the south. Barry walked to the corral gate and opened it wide, then turned to face Storm. "All right, big fella, you're free to go. I'll not keep you here against your will. Go on now. Git!" With clenched fists, he watched as the huge stallion plunged through the gate and went racing away. He stood watching as Storm crested the nearest rise and halted to send his neigh reverberating over the range.

Storm looked back from the top of the rise. He could see the boy standing beside the open corral gate. A gentle breeze wafted Barry's scent towards him. He pawed the ground impatiently. Then, swerving around, he raced down the hill towards the waiting boy. The moonlight shone on his red coat, changing it to a glowing fire. He looked like a burning comet streaking across the horizon.

He plunged up to the boy and, lowering his head, shoved it into the waiting arms of Barry. They stood in their embrace for a long time. Then Storm lifted his head and pawed the ground impatiently. As if in a daze, Barry mounted the huge stallion. This time there was no going back. Storm was free, and he was headed home carrying the boy he loved.

CHAPTER VIII
The Return of the Legend

Far to the south across the rugged Sierra Madres, señor Delgado watched another spring approach. He stood on his veranda looking listlessly over his valley. There was no hope in him anymore. He kept his eyes turned away from the stables on the east; the stables that had housed his Arabians and his gentle Surur. This year would have been the spring of Storm's fourth year. The championship race at Chihuahua would be held two weeks from now. With it would go the señor's last chance of redeeming his Arabians.

Later in the day, señor Delgado noticed a dust cloud coming up the valley. For a split second his heart skipped a beat as a thought flashed through his mind: could that dust, by some miracle, be Storm? But when the dust dispersed as the riders drew onto the grassland of the valley, the señor saw that it was his friendly rival, señor Gomez and his vaqueros.

Señor Gomez dismounted near the veranda and handed the lines of his mount to a vaquero. As he approached, señor Delgado could not help but feel bitterness towards the man who had held him to a foolish bet that was made in the heat of the moment. He rose to greet him. Señor Delgado, like Storm, had an aristocratic ancestry, and like Storm, he greeted his enemy with pride and dignity.

"Well, my friend, how are you faring?" inquired señor Gomez as he took an offered seat and accepted a glass of cold lemonade from the señor's house servant.

"Very good, thank you," replied the señor, "and you?"

"Ah, very well, I'm doing very well. My black stallion Diablo is coming along beautifully in his training. He will be impossible to beat in the race this year," he said.

"It is only two weeks off now, is it not?" asked the señor.

"Yes. You will be coming to watch the great event, will you not?" questioned señor Gomez.

"I do not think so. I am not getting any younger, and the race holds little interest for me anymore," he replied.

"So, your miracle horse has not returned, eh? It is as I said, he is probably long dead now," Gomez stated. "Even if he were to return, you would have no chance at winning the race now. It would be impossible to train a fully-grown stallion in two weeks' time, especially to handle all that will be expected of him in this race."

"I know, I know," replied señor Delgado.

"We have planned the course of the race," Gomez went on. "It will be long; a distance of seven miles. This distance includes two miles of a straight ordinary run. Then it begins to climb, over the foothills with brush jumps and rough terrain. Then a mile covered with undergrowth and trees, where, at the end is the Conchos River to cross. From the river, the course goes steeply up the mountain slopes to the rocky trails and thin mountain air. Then back down the mountain to reach the desert. The first part of the desert is sand dunes and hills—hot as Hades. The last part is back over the starting mile. It will enable one to watch the first and last part of the race."

"This course is longer and more difficult than ever before," said the señor.

"True, but I feel my Diablo has the training and the speed for it. In my back rangeland, we have been using him on the high hills and the rocky foothills. He is becoming used to it. I have a stretch of sand beach on which we are preparing him," replied Gomez.

"This race will take more than training," replied the señor. "It will take great heart and courage to run it. I should expect that most of the horses will finish slowly."

"Perhaps," said Gomez, "but this kind of terrain, this type of race, demands all the qualities for which an Arabian is famous. Their endurance, speed, heart, and courage. It will take intelligence too, to save something for the finish and not play themselves out in the rougher going."

"True, what you say is true," said the señor, "and you think your Diablo has these qualities in abundance? Training on hills is very different from climbing steep mountain slopes."

"Yes, but it is the most thorough training possible for any horse. He will win!" Gomez replied. "Wait and see!"

"I wish that my colt was back just to see if he would run this race well," mused the señor.

"Well, if he does come back, remember our last bet and give it a try anyway," laughed Gomez.

Storm and Barry were approaching the divide in the Sierra Madres that Storm had left two years ago. Barry, mounted on Storm, was wondering for the umpteenth time where they were going. They had travelled hundreds of miles in the last four months, coming steadily southward. Barry had been content to let Storm choose the direction of travel. It did not matter to him where they went, so long as they went together. He knew Storm was going someplace, somewhere. There was a definite design to the stallion's continuing one direction course. They had crossed the desert and for the first time, Storm headed directly up the slopes of the Sierra Madres. There was an added eagerness to his movement now and Barry sensed that the place to which Storm was headed was getting close.

In the weeks of being with Storm, the closeness between the boy and the stallion had grown. When Barry raced Storm over the ground, he became an extended part of the huge stallion. They understood each other completely. Barry knew he must never demand of the stallion; he must ask. Storm would obey him because he wanted to and because he loved the boy.

Storm stood at sixteen hands. He was fully developed, as his body was used to travelling in all kinds of terrain. Barry knew of the stallion's heart and courage, but even he could only guess at the greatness of the horse moving under him. Storm had never been asked to give it his all, so Barry did not know the strength that Storm encompassed.

They moved steadily across the divide in the mountains and descended the other side. As they reached the foothills and crested a rise, Barry saw the señor's valley spread out before them. Storm sent his ringing neigh across the valley and eagerly pawed the ground.

Young Juan was tending a small band of the señor's sheep when he heard the ringing bugle of the stallion. He looked up to see a moving ball of fire on the far hill. Storm neighed again. Dropping his staff, Juan raced towards the hacienda.

"Señor, señor, a miracle has happened! Firestorm has come home. Quick, quick! Come see!"

The señor was sitting on the front veranda. He stared at Juan through dazed eyes, not comprehending what the boy was saying.

"Come quick, señor. Storm has come home; I saw him! There, there he comes! See! It is Storm!" Juan frantically cried.

The señor could not believe his eyes. Coming towards him was a giant red horse. He seemed to float towards them like a moving flame. Then he, too, was moving forward. The peons came running from all over the ranchero. Each watched the approaching stallion with incredulous surprise.

Barry brought Storm to a stop in the courtyard. The señor approached slowly. He spoke to Storm in the musical language of his forebears. "Comma esta usta? Is it you? Is it really you, my colt? Yes, it is you, Storm. You have returned to us!" Storm lowered his head to nudge the señor playfully.

Any doubts Barry had about these people knowing his horse departed. He knew that the big stallion did not take to strangers. The señor then turned to the boy sitting astride Storm and with great dignity said, "You have returned my long-lost colt to us. He has grown into a very fine stallion. Step down, let us get to know each other. I am señor Delgado, I would like to hear about how you and Storm found each other. Perhaps I can also tell you something of this miracle that you have returned to us."

The señor heard Barry's story of how he had met and made friends with the young stallion.

"Texas, hmm... our Storm has travelled far in the last two years. I hope this Andy Dawson did not spoil him. Has he made him vicious?" the señor questioned Barry. "It did not seem so from the way he acted when you put him in the stables tonight, my son."

"He is not vicious, señor, but he does not like being told what to do. One must always ask of him, never demand," said Barry.

Barry heard the story of Storm's breeding and of the señor's Arabians. He learned of the foolish bet, and between the two, a deep liking was formed as they pieced together the story of Storm's two lost years.

They talked far into the night. When all was made clear, Barry found that by returning to Storm's home, he had also found a home for himself.

CHAPTER IX
The Legend Triumphs

In the days that followed, the activity on the ranchero picked up. The disused stable was repaired for the returned stallion. The peons worked hard now as their señor seemed to drop ten years from his age and became like his old self.

The orchards were pruned and the underbrush cleared. The grass was cut and the fountains cleaned to once again sprinkle the flowers in the courtyard. The gardens were tended to and the choked plants eagerly reached for the sun. The air of neglect and hopelessness that had fallen over the ranchero disappeared with the return of Storm.

The señor, with Barry beside him, joined in the hectic activity. They went together to the stables to see Storm, and the señor marvelled at how the horse had grown. It did not seem that his two years of freedom had hurt him. In fact, the señor had never seen a horse with such superb development. Barry told glowing tales of his speed. The señor knew that he would enter him in the race to be held in less than two weeks. He told Barry about the race, and what it entailed.

"It will not be enough to have great speed to win this race, it will also take great courage."

"Storm can do it, sir." Barry stated, his love and pride in the stallion throbbing in his voice.

"I think he may have a chance," agreed the señor, "for I feel his training has been more thorough than any that I could have given him." The señor continued, "We must leave soon to arrive at Chihuahua by the day of the race. Time has run out; the rest will be up to the fates."

"I only know that Storm will give all he has if you ask it of him," said Barry.

The señor ordered his vaqueros to be ready to leave the following morning. It would take less than a week to reach Chihuahua. They would arrive the night before the big race. The señor's people scurried about, making last-minute preparations for the long journey. They brought out their best serapes and sombreros. They knew that this time nothing would prevent Storm from running in the race. They looked forward to it with growing eagerness, for the giant red stallion had impressed them all with his beauty and fire. In some hearts, a tiny niggle of doubt persisted, as they all knew what would be demanded of the stallion in the race to come. Only the Lord could know if Storm was good enough, so in the small chapel, they lit candles before their patron saints and prepared to leave.

Barry had gone to his room early after bedding and checking in on Storm to make sure the stallion was all right. He went over everything in his mind. He thought of the journey to Chihuahua before them, and the running of the great race. He thought about the señor's foolish bet, realizing the hope that was growing in the señor's heart; the hope that Storm might recover his lost Arabians. Barry knew how much Storm's winning would mean to this gentle old man who had taken him in as a long-lost son. In the last few days, Barry felt a growing affection for the señor that he had not felt since his mother died. He prayed that the señor's hopes would be fulfilled. He knew the doubt the señor felt over Storm's remiss training and the superstitious feeling he had for the stallion's blood bay colouring. His last thought, as he drifted off to sleep, was who the señor would get to ride Storm in the race.

Five days later, the señor's cavalcade reached Chihuahua. They went directly to the starting place of the race where hundreds of people had gathered.

As soon as the señor had settled Storm in his allotted stall, he left Barry to find the judges to inform them of Storm's return and his intention to run him in the race.

A large crowd gathered to look at Storm. Here was a last-minute surprise for them. They looked with wonder upon this huge stallion and predicted trouble for señor Gomez' black Diablo.

Never had they seen such a colour in a horse. The sun reflected off his coat and turned it into flickering flames as he moved.

The tales of a beautiful red stallion quickly reached Pedro Gomez' encampment. He decided he would see who had entered this last-minute wonder horse. As he approached, he was surprised to see señor Delgado talking with a young, fair-haired boy. The boy was tall for his age and had the blue eyes of a typical American. Gomez drew up to the señor saying, "Well, well, so you decided to come and watch my black Diablo race after all, eh?"

"Meet a young friend of mine, Barry Stuart," the señor replied. "Barry, this is the señor Gomez I was telling you about."

Barry realized that this was the man who had taken advantage of the señor's pride. He felt an instant dislike for the man, "We did not come to watch your black stallion race, but to beat him," he said.

"Well," laughed Pedro Gomez, "the young cock crows mightily. With what do you expect to beat my horse with, a burro?"

"No, not a burro," replied the señor, "but with Storm. He has returned and will run in the race."

"Storm? Has returned?" Gomez repeated stupidly, then continued with disbelief, "let us see this miracle horse. I cannot believe what my ears hear you say."

Barry brought Storm forward. Gomez felt a small semblance of fear grow within him. Here was a truly magnificent piece of horseflesh. He swallowed, then regained his composure. He remembered his own black stallion, the years of training and good care he had received while this horse ran wild. There was no way he could know that Storm's training had been more thorough than any man could contrive. Gomez finally left them and returned to his own camp, pushing his doubt to the back of his mind.

The señor and Barry looked at Storm for a while, then walked to their tents for the night. As they approached the señor's tent, he asked Barry to come in for a minute.

"You know now what the race will be like. You have seen the map of the terrain. You realize what it would mean to me if Storm won. But, more importantly, is the fact that this race tests all the qualities of a purebred Arabian. Should Storm win, he would become the sire of more colts to come. The winner of this race will have much to do about the bettering of the breed."

"I realize the importance of the race, señor," Barry said, "and I think Storm can win."

"You have seen the other stallions. All magnificent pieces of horseflesh, all pure Arabians. They have all been well-trained over the last two years for this race. Tomorrow will answer all our questions," stated the señor. Then he continued slowly, from his heart, "I would like to ask you . . . if you would consent to ride Storm in the race? I have seen your love for him and his for you. I think you will get the best from him tomorrow. It will take his very best to win. Will you ride him for me?"

"Will I?" Barry's heart leaped, "Storm and I will give our best, I promise!"

The morning dawned clear and fine. At the judge's command, the horses were brought forward to the starting line. Barry was nervous. Sensing this, Storm pranced and jumped. Once he reared on his hind legs, bugling his challenge to the other stallions, but these were well-trained racehorses and they paid no attention to his call.

Approaching the starting line, Storm reared again. Barry brought him down, talking to him all the time. As Storm calmed down Barry felt his courage coming back. This was no different than riding Storm when they had been free. As they neared the starting post, the señor lifted his hand to Barry, then turned away. The time had come and now they were on their own. The judge lowered his hand. "They're off!" screamed the started. The race was on.

The riders on either side of Barry shouted to their horses as they leaped forward. Storm was left standing flat-footed. Sheer surprised kept them there as though frozen to the spot. Barry heard the tittering laughter of the spectators wash over him. Leaning forward, he called Storm, "Let's go, boy. It's come—the race! Run them down!" Storm leaped ahead as though shot from a cannon. From a standing start, he plunged to full speed, as Andy Dawson had taught him to do through the pain of the spur. Now he applied his powerful hindquarters to the same task that Barry had asked of him for love.

An amazed "Aaaah," arose from the spectators as they witnessed this tremendous exhibition of power and speed. Storm surged ahead, stretching out in an attempt to close the distance between himself and the six other stallions. With amazing speed, he narrowed the gap. At the end of the first mile, he caught and passed the first of them. He neighed challengingly as he forged by, then leveled out while gaining on the others in surges.

His strides were tremendous. To the wonder of the spectators lining the raceway, he proceeded to run the other stallions down as if they were standing still. Knowing horsemen looked upon this running horse, realizing they were witnessing one of the fastest horses of all times. They knew that in a short race, Storm would have easily been the winner, but this race had over five miles. They knew his speed must slacken. By the time he went through the rocky foothills, mountain slopes, and desert, he would have nothing left for the finish.

As the racing horses disappeared into the foothills with Storm well out in front, the señor turned away. He knew Barry had asked too much of Storm too soon. He should have been conserving strength for the long miles ahead.

Storm was running easily as the horses moved through the rocky, rough terrain of the foothills. Brush jumps loomed in their path. Barry slowed Storm. He was afraid the stallion might break a leg if he went too fast. The black stallion, Diablo, moved past them as Barry kept slowing Storm. Storm did not like being passed, but he listened to Barry's call and obeyed. He found this terrain no bother. He had become surefooted stampeding over surfaces like this with the wild bunch. They moved towards the Conchos River with Storm gaining ground on the black horse ahead of him.

Storm plunged into the river without hesitation, swimming steadily to the far side. After they crossed the river, Barry again asked the stallion to slow down. Storm shook his head furiously, not liking the tightened reins. The other stallions had gained slightly as they started up the mountainside. Diablo pulled farther and farther ahead. Storm had been running in these mountains for the past two years, his lungs were developed for work in the thin mountain air. Moving steadily upward, Storm closed the gap between Diablo and himself.

The black stallion rounded the turn and started to descent the mountain. The last two miles had taken its toll on the other stallions. Not one of them had been trained for this. Racing on hills was no preparation for high altitudes. Four long, hard miles were behind them. Diablo took heart again at the downhill going; he quickened his pace. Five other stallions dropped further behind the two front runners. Now only Storm was left to challenge the racing black.

Down the slope they galloped, straining every muscle in their bodies. Storm's surefootedness and familiarity with this kind of terrain had its own tale as he again drew upon the hard running black. As they came off the mountain and hit the loose sand dunes of the desert, Storm stumbled and almost fell, yet he quickly recovered and plunged forward again.

Barry knew now that he had pushed Storm too hard and too fast in those first miles. He was afraid that Storm would run himself into the ground before the last mile was covered.

He knew the courage it would take for his horse to hold himself together over this seemingly endless stretch.

Storm was breathing deeply and his red body was flecked with foam. Barry pulled him in, asking him to take a breather. Storm shook his head angrily. He saw the black moving ahead of him and shook his head at the continued holding. It was in the harsh desert that his kind had first been bred, and as he moved through the deep sand, it was the driving force of his desert ancestors behind him.

They came out of the desert with the last mile to the finish line ahead. A cry arose from the crowd lining the way as they caught sight of the two stallions approaching. They saw the black stallion of señor Gomez racing out in front. Surprise held them when they saw that the second horse was señor Delgado's Storm. The señor watched the oncoming horses with little hope. Here, at the finish, Storm would have nothing left to give after the way he had been running. He would go to pieces now, under the brutal demands of this last heart-breaking mile. He watched señor Gomez' Diablo surge forward again on the good footing, increasing his lead over Storm by another two lengths. Then he too screamed aloud.

The long hard miles were telling on Storm. He had given much in the first stretch. He still moved swiftly over the tough terrain. He was breathing hard. In vain, Barry tried to hold him in as they reached the easier footing of the last mile. This time Storm would not answer his demands to slow down. He saw the racing black stallion ahead of him and seemed to realize where he was and how much farther he still had to go. Relentlessly, he went after the running horse ahead. His head stretching forward and his ears were pricked as he moved ahead faster and faster. His strides became greater as he thundered down the hard-packed course. The wind roared in Barry's ears at the speed of his going, and he closed the gap between himself and the racing black.

People lining the course watched in awe as Storm proceeded to run Diablo down in the same way he had at the beginning of the race. His sweaty red body gleamed in the sun. He was a whirling firestorm that would consume all in its path. The peons' cries of "Firestorm, Firestorm!" were lost in the tumult.

With a quarter of a mile to go, Storm drew level with the hard-pressed black. Barry sat so still, asking nothing because his horse was giving everything. The two giant stallions raced neck and neck, matching stride for stride.

A hundred yards to go. Barry leaned ahead slightly and slapped Storm on the neck, calling to him one last time. Storm's great heart responded to the call. He rallied his tired muscles and from deep within came his body's call. With a tremendous surge of power, his strides lengthened and he moved past the black Diablo.

The huge crowd paid homage to Storm as they stood in respectful silence while he crossed the finish line. The winner by a dozen lengths.

Storm slowed of his own accord. He was very tired; his breath coming fast, but regularly. The señor pushed his way through the crowd and ran up to them. He looked with wondrous eyes upon this horse and the young boy who rode him. Then he led the giant red stallion forward to the victory circle.

Later at the barns, the señor informed the stunned Pedro Gomez that he would reclaim his Arabians the next week. They would bring them home where they belonged. El

Baroun, Surur, and all the rest. The dazed Gomez could only nod his head.

After the great crowds had left, the señor and Barry stood before Storm's stall. Their hearts overflowed with love for the great stallion. There was no need for words as they looked upon him.

"We will take him home tomorrow. From now on it will be his colts that do the running. If they inherit even part of his great heart and courage it will be enough. Here before us stands the greatest Arabian that was ever foaled," stated the señor.

Storm bugled his ringing challenge, then lowered his head to the boy beside him.

That is the legend of Storm. The peons still talk about it today; it has become part of their heritage. The story of Storm, and how he saved the valley and the señor's ranchero.

ACKNOWLEDGEMENTS

I would like to thank Trudy Binsfeld Okemow for the original cover illustration. Also Lani, Michelle and Donna for supplying photos and the original transcript of mom's book.

I would also like to thank Stephen Docksteader, Debbie Anderson and the editors and staff at FriesenPress press for their assistance in this project.

Thank you mom for writing this story for us!

—Stephen Radoux

Lightning Source UK Ltd.
Milton Keynes UK
UKHW011837100621
385314UK00001B/59